BAT
OUT THE
WINDOW

FIRST FLIGHT® is a registered trademark of Fitzhenry & Whiteside

Text copyright © 2001 by Sharon Jennings
Illustrations copyright © 2001 by John Mardon

Published in Canada by Fitzhenry & Whiteside,
195 Allstate Parkway, Markham, Ontario L3R 4T8

Published in the United States by Fitzhenry & Whiteside,
121 Harvard Avenue, Suite 2, Allston, Massachusetts 02134

10 9 8 7 6 5 4 3 2 1

National Library of Canada Cataloguing in Publication Data

Jennings, Sharon
Bats out the window

(A first flight level four reader)
(A first flight chapter book)
ISBN 155041-678-2

I. Mardon, John II. Title. III. Series. IV. Series: A first flight chapter book.

PS8569.E563B38 2001   jC813'.54   C2001-901083-4
PZ7.J429877Ba 2001

U.S. Cataloging-in-Publication Data

Jennings, Sharon.
Bats out the window : a first flight level four reader / by Sharon Jennings ;
illustrated by John Mardon. –1st ed.
[56] p. : ill. ; cm. – (A first flight chapter book)
Summary: Sam and Simon are rescued from the most
boring summer ever when a movie crew comes to town.
IBSN 1-55041-6782 (pbk.)
1. Friends – Fiction. 2. Summer – Fiction. I. Mardon, John, ill. II. Title. III. Series.
[E] 21   2001 AC CIP

Fitzhenry & Whiteside acknowledges with thanks
the Canada Council for the Arts, the Government of Canada
through the Book Publishing Industry Development Program (BPIDP),
and the Ontario Arts Council for their support of our publishing program.

Design by Wycliffe Smith

A First Flight® Level Four Reader

BATS OUT THE WINDOW

By Sharon Jennings
Illustrated by John Mardon

Fitzhenry & Whiteside

For Paulette at Fifty.
S.J.

CHAPTER ONE

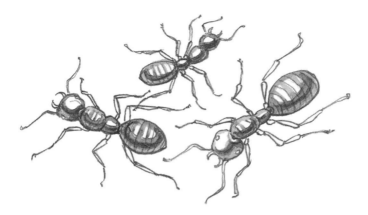

Simon and I were lying under the sprinkler watching ants get wet.

"This is really boring," I said. "This is the most boringest thing I've ever done in my whole life. Let's go to the park."

"Shhh!" said Simon. "I'm trying to count. Fifty-seven, fifty-eight...."

So I said, "Forty-nine, sixty-six, one hundred and three...."

So Simon punched me in the arm.

So I grabbed his leg and dragged him across the grass.

So he kicked me with his other leg and knocked me down. We rolled around a bit, and then Simon said, "Oh, all right. Let's go to the park."

The park isn't any big whoop or anything. But it has a wading pool with a fountain that spouts water.

"Tag!" I yelled at Simon. "You're it!" And I took off around the pool.

"Ewwww!" Someone screamed. "Stop splashing!"

I turned to look. It was Margaret. I hadn't seen her since school ended. I didn't want to see her now.

"It's a pool, you know," I informed her. "You're supposed to get wet."

"Not by you, you little worm. I'm telling." And she did.

So the lifeguard, who is just Ben's older brother, came over.

"Any more splashing and you're out!"

What a showoff. He just wants all the girls to think he's really special.

"Come on, Simon. Let's play sharks and sneak up on the little kids."

So we tried that. We swam to the deep water in the middle — but it's only just up to our belly buttons — and we waved our hands

around like a shark's fin and bumped into kids underwater.

Soon a bunch of kids were crying and calling to their moms, and Ben's older brother stomped up to us again.

"What's with you guys?"

"We weren't splashing," said Simon.

"Time out!" yelled Ben's older brother. "Go sit on the edge of the pool for five minutes."

Like he's a teacher or something.

So Simon and I went and sat on the edge, only we kept sticking our toes in the water whenever Ben's older brother wasn't looking.

Then I looked around and noticed that all the babies play in the water at the edge. Then I noticed that all the babies had diapers sticking out from under their bathing suits.

"Simon. Do you think there's anything in those diapers?" I asked.

Simon started counting.

"There's seventeen babies at this pool. Some of them must have something in their diapers."

"Ewwww!" I said. I sounded just like Margaret. "I'm out of here."

And in five minutes, Simon and I were back in my yard, lying under the sprinkler, watching ants get wet.

It wasn't fair. The summer started off so great, and now there was nothing to do and no one to play with. And it was really, really hot.

"This is the most boringest summer ever!" I said.

And just then we saw my mom waving a piece of paper with one hand and waving at us with the other hand and yelling something.

She turned off the sprinkler and came marching across the yard.

CHAPTER TWO

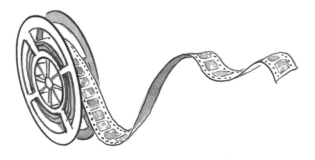

"Guess what?!" my mom demanded. "Come on, guess! Guess!"

Simon went first.

"You won a trip and I can go too?" he asked.

"Did we win something, Mom?" I asked. "A million dollars?"

My mom shook her head. "Nope and nope," she said.

"Tickets!" I yelled. "You got us tickets to the Fungus concert!"

That kind of changed my mom's mood.

"Sam. You are not going to the Fungus concert. For the tenth time. Okay?"

I sighed. "Then what is it?" And I began jumping up and down, trying to get the letter out of my mom's hand.

My mom smiled and showed us.

It didn't look too interesting to me. I mean, it was a long letter and it wasn't addressed to me. It just said, "Dear Occupant." I began reading. But Simon is a better reader than me, and he finished first and yelled right in my ear.

"Sam! A movie! They're making a movie on your street!"

I stared at Simon and then kept on reading. It was true. And not just any movie.

"Barry Adams!" I yelled back in Simon's ear. "Barry Adams is in the movie!" He's been in six movies and he's only nine. I bet I'm his biggest fan.

I kept on reading 'cause I wanted to know when we'd get to meet him and if we'd get to be in the movie. But that's not why they sent the letter. They sent it just to let us know that, next week, lots of trailers and trucks would be parked up and down our street. They hoped we wouldn't mind and wouldn't get too upset with all the noise.

Whoop.

"What's so good about this?" I asked.

My mom rolled her eyes. "Sam. There's going to be a film crew and movie stars on our street. They are actually filming in a house up the road. Barry Adams will be here. Maybe you can meet him. At least you'll have something to do for a few days."

"Yeah, Sam,"" said Simon. "We can watch and take pictures and maybe get everybody's autograph. We can tell everybody all about it. It'll be cool."

"Think about it, Sam," said my mom.

So I thought about it. And what I thought was that it sounded a lot better than watching ants under the sprinkler.

The next few days were kind of weird on our street. Big trucks showed up and people began fixing the fronts of some of the houses. Four houses on our side and four houses on the other side. They put pink and purple awnings out over the living room windows and painted doors and stuck in different flowers.

Simon banged on my door one morning early and came in for breakfast.

"I went up the street first thing and found out all about it," he said. "The movie takes place in New York City in the fifties."

"Simon. This is Canada. And the fifties were a long time ago."

Simon rolled his eyes just like my mom does.

"It's a movie, stupid! They're pretending!"

I was going to tell Simon he was a know-it-all, but I wanted to find out what else he knew before I called him a know-it-all.

"And it's all about spies and secret agents and Barry Adams plays a kid who finds out a big secret about his neighbors, who are just pretending to be neighbors and then his life is in danger."

"How'd you find out all this?" I asked.

"I asked the guys doing the fixing on those houses. They work for a company that only works for movies. They change your house. And when the movie's done, they fix your house up again. Only better."

"So why didn't they pick my house?" I asked.

"They needed a house with an attic so they could stick a spy telescope and stuff out the attic window."

"It isn't fair," I said. "The man who lives in that attic house is real mean. He never says hi or nothing. Mr. Kuzak just yells if I run across his grass. And then he sprays me with the hose by accident on purpose." I explained all this to Simon because he just

moved in five weeks ago. He doesn't know all the neighbors like I do.

"What's really not fair is that Barry Adams will be in his house," said Simon.

I scowled. "Stupid old Mr. Kuzak probably doesn't even know who Barry Adams is."

Simon sighed. "Well, at least we'll be able to see Barry Adams. And take pictures. And we might be able to meet him. We're famous too, you know."

"Oh yeah, right!" I said. ""What are we going to do? Give him our autographs?!"

"Sam. We caught a couple of burglars and got our pictures in the paper. How many kids have done that?"

Maybe Simon was right.

"I'm going back," he said. "Are you coming or not?"

Well, of course I was coming. For a know-it-all, Simon sometimes doesn't know much.

CHAPTER FOUR

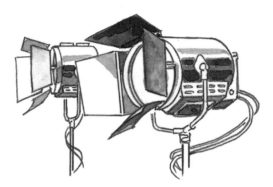

We left my house at the same time as some big, and I mean BIG, trailers showed up. Nine of them, all clean and white, were trying to park up and down the street, blocking everybody's driveways.

And further up the street, lots of people were walking around, doing stuff and looking busy. Then Simon and I saw the cars.

It was unbelievable! Seven old cars from the fifties, really long and wide and with big tail fins and painted pink or turquoise or red. And they had New York license plates. Then Simon pointed to something, and I saw that they had even changed our street signs. I live on Pinehill Avenue, but now it was Lincoln Road!

"You stay here," said Simon. "I'm running home for my camera."

So I stood and watched as all these people rolled out huge lights and camera cables from the trucks. I was wondering if Barry Adams was around anywhere and thought maybe I should ask.

"Hey! Hey, kid!" someone yelled.

Then this guy with a huge belly and a small T-shirt stepped in front of me. I mean, I had to tilt my head back to see his face over his belly.

"Sorry, kid. This is as far as you go." And he stood there with his arms folded. He had a lot of weird tattoos on both arms.

"But I'm Barry Adams' biggest fan," I told him.

"Yeah, yeah. That's what they all say. Back!"

Then I noticed the wooden blockades up around the fixed-up houses. Some of my neighbors were leaning on them, watching what was going on. The big guy pointed back the way I had come. I decided not to argue with him.

I turned around and saw Simon. He had two cameras around his neck and was carrying his video equipment.

I told him what had happened.

"You mean this is as close as we get? How are we supposed to get a picture of Barry Adams? He'll look like an ant from this far away!"

So I pointed out the guy with the belly and tattoos.

"Oh." Simon sighed and looked around. Then he grabbed my arm and yelled.

"Look, Sam! It's Officer Green!"

I looked to where he was pointing.

"Yeah, so what?" I asked.

But Simon was already heading for the police cruiser.

CHAPTER FIVE

"Well, well!" exclaimed Officer Green. "If it isn't my two favorite heroes!"

Officer Green was one of the police who came to our backyard the night we caught the burglars.

Simon smiled at him. "What are you doing here?" he asked.

"They've hired some off-duty cops to hang around here. Make sure some crazy fans don't try anything weird." And he looked right at me when he said it. I don't know why he didn't look at Simon. With three cameras, Simon was the one who looked like a crazy fan.

"We were hoping to get a bit closer," said Simon.

"Well, I tell you what. You stick close to me and I'll see what I can do."

"You mean it?! Gosh, thanks!"

So we stuck close to Officer Green all day long. We took turns running home to go to the bathroom, and we took turns running home to get lunch. In the afternoon, I spotted mean old Mr. Kuzak.

"Hey, Mr. Kuzak," I called. He probably would have ignored me, but he saw Simon and me standing beside Officer Green, and came right over.

I figured he remembered that we were heroes. I figured wrong.

"These little stinkers causing problems, officer?" he asked, giving us a dirty look.

"Not at all, sir," said Officer Green. "They're two of the best lads I know."

"Hmmph!" snorted Mr. Kuzak. "Well, just keep them away from my house. I wouldn't want anything to happen to your precious lads."

"Now, what do you mean by that?" asked Officer Green.

"Nothing. But there's a lot of insurance on my house because of this movie. I'm just warning them not to get into trouble." And he gave us another nasty look.

With Officer Green there, I felt brave enough to ask a question. "Have you seen Barry Adams? Is he really in your house?"

"Barry, shmarry," he said. "I could care less. They're paying me big bucks to rent my house and they're paying me to stay in a hotel. And now that I've handed over my keys, that's where I'm going." He snorted again and left.

"This isn't fair," I said. "He gets Barry Adams and money!"

"Well, I hope they pay him enough to get rid of those dopey white shoes," Simon said.

And we both looked at Mr. Kuzak's shoes and laughed.

Officer Green told us to mind our manners.

At dinnertime Simon's mom was really nice and brought us some pizza.

And then it was dark and we still hadn't seen Barry Adams.

And then all these really bright lights got turned on, and it was just like daytime. Some actors we didn't know showed up, and the director yelled quiet. We watched the actors have a fight and run into the attic house. Then we watched them come out and fight and run into the house again. Then we watched them do it four more times! Finally, the director was happy and said everybody could quit for the day.

"That's it, boys," said Officer Green. "Better luck tomorrow."

So Simon and I went back to my house. And you'll never guess what happened.

CHAPTER SIX

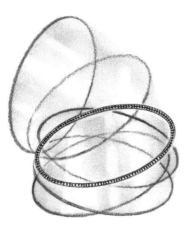

"What?!" I yelled.

"You heard me," said Ellen. "I'm in the movie."

"Neat," said Simon.

First I glared at Simon, then I glared at my little sister.

"How did you get in the movie?" I asked her.

"I was just skipping by one of those trailers and a lady came out and asked me to be in the movie. She said I was cute."

"Neat," said Simon again.

So I glared at him again.

"Does Mom know?"

"Of course Mom knows. I had to go home and get her. Then we went to a wardrobe trailer and I got to pick out a poodle skirt."

"A what?"

"A poodle skirt. It's pink and round and swirls when I swirl. And tomorrow I get a perm."

"A what?" I said again.

"A perm. My hair's going to be all curly so I look like a fifties girl. That's what the lady said."

"So Simon and I waited all day long and nothing happened, and you just get to be in the movie for no good reason?"

"I told you the lady said I was cute!" Ellen shouted.

"What do you have to do?" asked Simon.

"Well, I have to stand out in front of Mr. Kuzak's house playing with a hula hoop. I had to show them that I could hula hoop, and I can, so that's why I got the part. And...ta dah!...they're paying me two hundred dollars."

"Neat!" said Simon for the third time.

Then Ellen showed us the hula hoop that they gave her to practice with.

"Give me that," I said. And I tried to hula hoop, but the stupid hoop wouldn't hula and just kept dropping to the floor.

So Simon tried it and of course he was good at it, and he and Ellen were laughing

their heads off and having a really good time.

I was getting madder and madder.

"This isn't fair!" I finally exploded. "Barry Adams is my favorite movie star. I'm his biggest fan, and you get to be in his movie and make money!"

Ellen smirked. "When I see Barry, I'll get you his autograph."

Then Simon said, "Maybe we'd better get your autograph, Ellen. You're going to be famous!"

Then they both laughed some more and I gave them both dirty looks, but they just ignored me.

"I'm going to bed," I said. "You two can do what you want."

But they weren't even listening to me, so I just stomped off to my room and slammed the door.

CHAPTER SEVEN

Simon called on me first thing next morning. It was still dark outside.

"Come on, Sam. Wake up. We've got to be first on the set."

'On the set' is film talk and we were getting good at it. And Simon was right. We didn't want to waste any time. If we were going to meet Barry or be in the movie, we had to be the first people hanging around.

So we grabbed two bowls of cereal and ran up the street, trying not to spill any.

We saw Officer Green as soon as we got there. He was talking to the director we watched all last night. And no one else was around.

"Come here, you two," he called.

Then the director shook our hands and told us her name was Sally.

"I've been hearing great things about you," she said. "And I think it would be a real pleasure for Barry Adams to meet a couple of real-life heroes."

Simon and I stood there staring at her with our mouths open.

"Wow!" Simon finally said.

"Yeah. Wow!" I said too. Just wait 'til I told Ellen.

"Barry's going over his lines right now. But I'll send someone to get you in about an hour."

I didn't know how Simon and I were going to get through the next hour. But Officer Green made us eat our bowls of cereal and then sent us home to brush our teeth and wash our hands.

"And come back in some clean T-shirts!" he yelled. Geesh! Like he was our parents!

So there we were, looking all 'spiffy', as my Grandma says, when the security guy with the tattoos came to get us.

"You two Sam and Simon?" he asked.

We nodded.

"Yeah, well, I'm Mortimer. Follow me. And don't call me Mort."

"Have fun, boys!" said Officer Green. "And don't do anything stupid."

We followed Mortimer along the sidewalk to one of the big trailers. He pointed to the door and said, "In there. And don't do anything stupid."

Simon and I went up the steps and stuck our heads inside.

Barry Adams was there talking to Sally. Barry Adams. Right there. Standing in front of us. Barry Adams.

"Come on in," Sally said. "Sam and Simon live just down the road. They helped catch some burglars this summer and they're just dying to meet you."

Barry Adams shook our hands and said hi. We said hi back, and then I said, "I'm your biggest fan."

Barry rolled his eyes.

"Give me your camera, Simon," Sally said, "I'll take some pictures of the three of you."

Barry put his arms around us like we were his best friends. We all smiled, and then Sally left us alone.

I wanted to ask Barry about what it was like to be a big movie star, but Simon started first.

"Do you miss your friends?" he asked.

What a dopey question.

Barry shook his head. "I don't really have friends. I'm always traveling."

"What about school? You've got friends there."

"Nope. I get teachers on the set. I guess Mortimer's my best friend."

I shuddered.

"Simon's my best friend," I said. "But just since five weeks ago. He moved here and we made a club called the Bats and we ended up scaring away some burglars."

"Nothing like that ever happens to me," said Barry.

"But you're a movie star. Stuff like that happens to you all the time," I pointed out.

"Not for real. It's all pretend."

So then Simon showed Barry how to make the Bats' secret handshake. They linked thumbs and wiggled their eight other fingers like bat wings.

"We'll write you if you want," said Simon. "We'll show you our secret code." Then he showed Barry how to write his name. Like this: arryb.

"And I'm nimos and he's mys."

And when Sally came back in, Barry asked if we could follow him around for the day while he was shooting.

"Please, Sally?" he said. Like he really meant it.

Sally said yes.

CHAPTER EIGHT

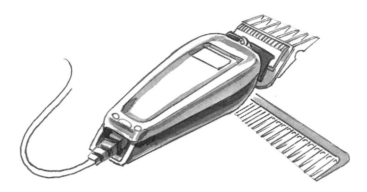

So we watched Barry get his head shaved
so he looked like one of those dorks in
early black and white TV shows. He had to
do this every day so his head looked just
right all the time. Then we watched Barry
get his make-up done, and we watched
Barry talking to Sally and to a whole bunch
of other people.

And then we stood behind Sally and a
whole bunch of cameras, and we watched
Barry say his lines fifty times until Sally
was happy.

Then it was lunchtime.

"What if we have to stand here and

watch Barry eat?" Simon whispered.

But maybe someone heard him or heard my stomach growling, 'cause someone said we could eat lunch too.

It was really weird. One whole trailer was there just as a kitchen, and all these people did nothing but cook all day so nobody had to waste time looking for a restaurant. And the food was really fancy. Not hot dogs or anything. I said so to Barry and he sighed.

"Yeah. Too fancy." And he sighed again.

And then Simon said, "Can you come to my house for lunch?"

I started to laugh. Sometimes Simon's so dumb.

But Barry said, "You mean it? I'll ask."

And while I stood there with my mouth open, Barry got permission to eat at Simon's.

"You be back in one hour and don't do anything stupid," Sally said.

Why does everyone keep saying that to us?!

So we ran down the street to my house and we showed Barry how to walk the fence to Simon's backyard.

"Mom! Mom! This is Barry Adams! He wants lunch!""

And so Simon's mom made us peanut butter-and-jam sandwiches because that's what Barry wanted. And we had plain old white milk because that's what Barry wanted too. I even ate all my carrot sticks because they're Barry's favorite.

And then we went outside and we showed Barry the climber we used as our Bat Club and we showed him our pictures of the night we caught the burglars.

"Hey! said Barry. "I've got a great idea! Let's act the whole thing out! I'll be the burglar and I'll sneak up on you and you can be you!"

So we gave Barry some rotten garbage from the composter at the back of the yard. He threw it at us and we soaked him with the hose. It was really fun.

And then Mortimer showed up and yelled at us.

"Everyone's looking for you! You're late!" And he glared at Barry. Then he glared at us. "And I told you two not to do anything stupid!"

"Aw, come on, Mortimer," said Barry.

"We were just having fun. And Sam and Simon are really great actors. I think they should be in the movie."

Simon and I looked at each other. Even Simon's mouth was hanging open this time.

And then Mortimer was glaring at us again.

"You two want to be in the movie?"

"Yes!" we both shouted.

"Hmmm. Well, first thing, see, you gotta get your hair cut right. You gotta get crew cuts like Barry's. And I'm the barber, see?"

We saw. We didn't like it.

"Mortimer's just fooling," laughed Barry. "We have a real barber on the set. Come on. I'll tell Sally to let you be extras. You'll have to go to wardrobe and make-up."

I thought about Ellen and I had to ask. "Do we get paid?"

"Yeah, but not much. Maybe two hundred a day," said Barry.

Two hundred a day! For that much money, I'd let Mortimer do anything he wanted to my hair!

CHAPTER NINE

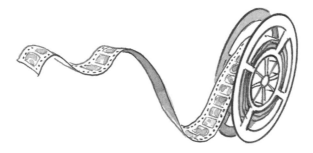

So after our moms came and signed some papers, Simon and I had to go to the make-up trailer. First they shaved our heads. Boy, did we look dorky.

"Smile!" said Simon. And he took my picture.

Then they put some make-up on us.

"Am I gonna look like a girl?" I asked.

But the make-up artist said it was just so we wouldn't look really sick under bright lights.

"Smile!" said Simon again, and took another picture of me.

"Give me that!" I yelled and reached for the camera.

"Oops! Sorry, Sam. There's only one picture left. Better save it for something really good."

I scowled at him.

Then we went to the wardrobe trailer. They gave us jeans and T-shirts and old-fashioned running shoes.

"Don't we get a costume?" I asked.

"This ain't The Wizard of Oz, kid," said Mortimer. "Jeans and high tops is your costume."

"Oh."

"Okay. Now I'm going to take you to watch Barry some more. And when they finish inside the house, we go outside and shoot you." And Mortimer laughed.

"He means shoot our scene, don'tcha, Mortimer?" said Simon.

Mortimer smirked. "Just hang around and be ready when they call you."

So Mortimer marched us into mean old Mr. Kuzak's house. It was weird and neat at the same time. I knew Mr. Kuzak would be really mad if he knew Simon and I were in there.

We followed everyone upstairs and up into the attic. There wasn't much room, so Simon and I had to stay way at the back.

"This isn't any good," I complained. "We can't see hardly nothing."

Simon agreed.

"Come on, Sam," he said. "The next scene's in the big bedroom. We can get in there now and get a good spot."

We hurried down the hall. No one was around.

And then Simon had an idea.

"Sam!" he said, pointing at the bed. "We could hide under there and no one would know! We'd be in the movie and no one would know but us! It'd be like we were spys in a spy movie!"

"Are you nuts?! We'd get caught for sure!"

And just then, I could hear voices. The crew was on its way.

"See?" I said. "We'll be caught."

Simon smiled at me.

"Chicken," he said.

"Am not!"

"Chicken." And he started making chicken noises.

I punched him on the arm. So he grabbed my arm and pulled.

And in seconds we were both under mean old Mr. Kuzak's bed.

CHAPTER TEN

And just in time!

Soon the cameras and crew were in the bedroom and Sally was explaining what she wanted.

I pinched Simon's arm and I made a terrible face, but of course it was too dark for Simon to see how mean I looked.

But then the lights came up really bright and Simon began to laugh when he looked at me.

"You look like you pooped your pants!" he whispered.

And so we waited and listened from under the bed. I started thinking about how I'd get even with Simon. But then I started thinking about how Simon and I could go to this movie when it came out, and we'd be the only ones who knew we were in this part of the movie. And then I thought about how, when I was famous, I'd tell everybody about what I'd done, because when I was famous, nobody would yell at me.

So I listened to all the lines that everybody said so I'd remember the part.

"Ya wanna live, yer gonna havta jump
outa the window."

And we waited and waited and listened
and listened on and on and on.

No one was doing anything right. Sally
was yelling at everybody. I think they were
up to take 357, and my right arm and both
feet were asleep, and I had to go to the
bathroom.

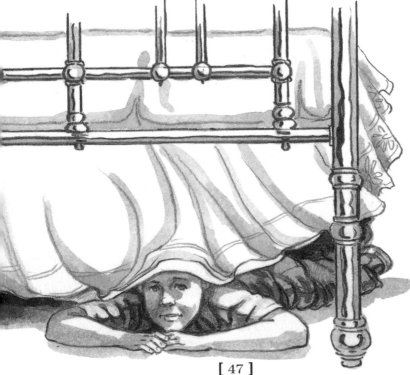

"Ya wanna live, yer gonna havta jump outa the window."

How many times could the bad guy say that line? How many times could he head over to the window? The window had all been changed around so it could open easily and Barry could jump out. Well, not Barry, exactly, but Barry's stunt double. But they never got around to that part. And that would have been the fun part because the stunt guy would get to land on a sort of trampoline down below.

"Ya wanna live, yer gonna havta jump outa the window."

And then I heard the weirdest little noise coming from Simon. I turned to look. He was snoring! He was asleep!

I thought of those huge dinosaur-hiccup snores my dad does, and I knew we'd be caught for sure if Simon could snore like my dad! Boy! If Simon could snore like my dad, my dad would probably hear it down the street!

I saw Simon's mouth puckering up and getting ready to let out another noise. I thought about covering his mouth with my arm, but my right arm was closest to him and it was asleep. And I knew I couldn't move it fast enough.

And then, just when I thought we were goners, Sally yelled. "Cut!" which covered up Simon's whistle-snore. And then, when everybody was moving around, I managed to wake Simon up without scaring him so he wouldn't jump up and bang his head on the bed.

It seemed to take forever to get everybody out of the room.

"What time is it?" I asked Simon.

He peered at his watch. "Eight."

"Eight?! We're going to be in big trouble!"

"Why? Everybody knows we're up here with Barry. No one's looking for us," he pointed out.

I figured Simon was probably right, and the two of us slid out from under the bed.

And slid right back under just as fast!

Sally came back into the room and pointed out some things she didn't like to someone else, and she said maybe that's why the scene wasn't working. So all of a sudden more people showed up and started moving things around, and I didn't know what Simon and I were going to do if they decided to move the bed too.

And then Sally said dinner break had been long enough, and everybody got called back up to the bedroom for another round of shooting.

And so, we lay there, hour after hour, getting stiff and sore. And hungry! My stomach was starting to make so much noise I thought it would be as bad as my dad's snores! I looked around under the bed, but nothing was there. That's the trouble with adults. Under my bed there would have been lots of leftover stuff to eat.

More time passed and I was bored like I had never been bored before. And I thought I could never go to see this movie.

I'd scream if I heard these lines one more time.

"Ya wanna live, yer gonna havta jump outa the window."

I started thinking that watching ants under the sprinkler hadn't been so bad after all.

CHAPTER ELEVEN

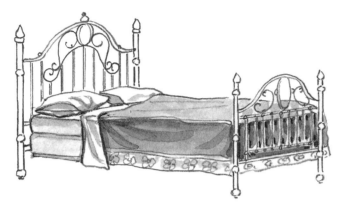

I was dreaming that I was being chased by
spys down Pinehill Avenue, and I kept
shouting, "Jump outa the window! I wanna
live!"

And then Simon was shaking me, and I
remembered mean old Mr. Kuzak's bed, and
then I realized I was still under mean old
Mr. Kuzak's bed!

"Sam! Sam! Wake up! It's three in the
morning!"

Three!

"Why aren't your parents looking for
us?" I asked Simon.

"Why would they? I told them we're

sleeping in your tent."

Oh oh.

"I told my parents I was sleeping in the bathouse," I said.

Simon sighed. "We're gonna be in big trouble," he said.

Simon and I crawled out from under the bed and stood up. We stretched and groaned and yawned.

We were at the stairs and starting down. We weren't sure if there were any guards around so we weren't making a lot of noise. We didn't want to have to explain anything to Mortimer, or anyone else.

And a good thing too, because all of a sudden we heard a creaky noise from the kitchen and heard a door open.

We turned and ran back upstairs.

"Under the bed!" hissed Simon.

"No!" I hissed back.

But there was nowhere else to go.

I crawled under and banged my head on something.

"It's your camera," I whispered, and hung it around my neck.

We both wiggled around until we were

facing out. Then we were very quiet and very still. Once again we waited and listened.

Someone came up the stairs and stood in the doorway. Whoever it was had a flashlight. Then the light moved down the hall to another room.

"Why would a security guard sneak around in the dark with just a flashlight?" Simon asked.

I started feeling really sick. And then whoever it was came back to the doorway and into the bedroom. And came right over to the bed.

And then I saw it. Poking in under the bedskirt. The tip of a white shoe. A dopey white shoe. And I wiggled a bit further back, forgetting about the camera underneath me. I stopped moving and held my breath as I heard the camera click.

And, at the same time, Mr. Kuzak coughed and his white shoe moved. We heard him leave the room.

"Oh, man," whispered Simon. "That was close!"

"What's he doing here?" I whispered

back.

"It's his house, stupid!"

But this time, Simon wasn't such a know-it-all. Because soon we heard something splashing, and then we smelled gasoline. Then we heard Mr. Kuzak go downstairs and out the door. We scrambled out from under the bed and I started to go to the stairs.

"Sam! No! Not that way! We have to get out the window!"

We rushed to the window, and I showed Simon that it was fake and could push out. I grabbed his arm and...you'll never guess what I said to him.

"Ya wanna live, yer gonna havta jump outa the window!"

And out we flew down to the trampoline. Then we bounced off and took off down the road.

And minutes later, mean old Mr. Kuzak's house went up in flames.

CHAPTER TWELVE

Simon and I stopped running three doors down the street. Security guards were all over the place, and soon we heard sirens. The fire engines showed up at the same time that someone shone a flashlight on us.

"Here they are!" yelled a security guard. And then three men grabbed Simon and me by the arms.

"Wait! What are you doing?" I yelled.

And then Mr. Kuzak was there and yelling too.

"I knew you two were a couple of stinkers!" he screamed. "You belong in jail!"

"What?! Wait! No!" But no one was listening to us.

And then our parents showed up and began yelling.

"How could you do something so stupid?!" yelled my father.

"Sam, you are grounded for the rest of your life!" yelled my mother.

"Simon, you are never leaving the house ever again!" yelled Simon's father.

Simon's mom started to yell something too, but a security guard yelled first.

"Quiet! These two boys were seen starting the fire. They'll be lucky if they don't spend the rest of their lives in jail! The police are on their way."

"But he started it!" I yelled, and I pointed to mean old Mr. Kuzak.

"Liar!" he yelled back. "I'm going to sue you and see you in jail!"

"You're the liar!" I yelled back.

And then Simon looked around and grabbed my arm.

"Look! Officer Green!"

And Simon and I broke free from the guards and ran to Officer Green. And he took us off by ourselves and told everyone to stay back and to stop yelling.

We told him everything.

"And you're sure it was Mr. Kuzak?" he asked.

"Yes," said Simon. "We saw his shoe, his dopey white shoe. We...." And he stopped talking and did this thing he does when he's thinking really hard.

He closed his eyes tight and started making funny faces. And then he opened his eyes and yelled.

"The camera! Sam! The camera!"

It took me a second, but then I remembered.

"I had it when we jumped," I said. "It must have come off my neck when we jumped."

And the three of us ran back to the house. Of course we couldn't get near, but Officer Green spoke to someone. Then a couple of people looked all around the bushes where the trampoline was.

"Here it is!" And they brought Simon's camera over. It was kind of smashed up, but the film looked okay.

And a couple of hours later, Officer

Green was holding a picture of Mr. Kuzak's dopey white shoe poking under the bed. It didn't take the police long to find an empty can of gasoline a couple of streets away. Mr. Kuzak's fingerprints were all over it. It turned out he had put lots of insurance on his house so he'd get lots of money when it burned down. Then he'd sue the movie company for more money.

When they took him off to jail, he was still calling me and Simon 'dirty little stinkers'.

CHAPTER THIRTEEN

So Simon and I got to be heroes a second
time and got our pictures in the paper
again. But this time it was better because
they took our picture with Barry Adams
instead of with the mayor.

And the movie studio was so happy with
us that they sent us off to Wonderville with
Barry. We got to spend a whole day on rides
and waterslides and eating all the junk food
we wanted. Mortimer took us and he turned
out to be lots of fun.

"You can be in the Bat Club too," I told
him.

"Yeah," said Barry. "Your code name's rumotrim!"

I guess the only bad thing was that we didn't get to be in the movie. They had done the crowd scenes when Simon and I were sleeping under Mr. Kuzak's bed.

But a few months later, when the movie came out, we were given special passes to go see it.

It was a really great movie, except for the part where there was a close-up of Ellen doing the hula-hoop thing in some dorky looking skirt. People sitting around us knew Ellen, and clapped.

Then suddenly we were in
mean old Mr. Kuzak's bedroom.
I grabbed Simon's arm.
"The bed! It's us!"
"Shhhh!" everyone hissed.
Hmmmph! I didn't get to be in
the movie and now everyone
was telling me to be quiet.
I decided to show
them who was boss.
"Sam," whis-
pered Simon.
"Don't do anything
stupid!"
"Don't worry,"
I told him.
So I waited, and I
waited, and just at the
right moment, I stood up
and yelled out, "Ya wanna
live, yer gonna havta jump
outa the window!"
I got kicked out of the theatre,
but I didn't care.
Sometimes you just have to do
something stupid.

SECRET BAT CODE

I asked Simon if it was okay with him that I tell you our secret code, and he said okay. So here it is.

First you have to swap vowels. Like this:

a = y

e = u

i = o

So if your name is Gary, you'd write Gyra. Except that Simon and I decided to make it a bit harder and so you have to write your name backwards. Gary is aryg. Simon is nimos. My name, Sam, is mys. My sister Ellen is nullu.

You can write notes to your friends, but don't let anyone else know.

ubaym uni ayd eia nyc noij uht tyb belc.